The Christmas Wish Tree

MONTGOMERY THOMPSON

THE CHRISTMAS WISH TREE

Copyright © 2015 Montgomery Thompson

All rights reserved.

ISBN: 1979079536
ISBN-13: 978-1979079532

DEDICATION

To my family, all of them…ever.

THE CHRISTMAS WISH TREE

ACKNOWLEDGEMENTS

Edited by Amanda Meuwissen
Associate Editor Willow Wood

MONTGOMERY THOMPSON

THE CHRISTMAS WISH TREE

Chapter 1

The perfect day flashed by Martin's window in a kaleidoscope of sun sparkled whites and greens. His father drove and his mother chatted away next to him, leaving Martin the whole back seat to himself. He was eager to get home and start decorating. Their Christmas tree was safely lashed to the roof as they sped along. Martin pressed his face up against the cold glass of the window, trying to catch a glimpse of the boughs that danced in the wind. It was the last thing he remembered before waking up.

"Martin?"
It sounded like his Aunt Dottie.
"Martin honey it's okay. Wake up now, we'll get you some tea."
It was definitely Aunt Dottie, tea seemed to be her cure for everything. His neck throbbed painfully and the side of his face felt numb. "Wha – where am I?"
"You're in the hospital honey. You were in a terrible car accident, poor dear."
Martins eyes fluttered, he couldn't stay awake no matter how hard he tried. "Aunt… Dottie?..."
"Just rest dear, you're going home with me."

***

"He's smaller than Dottie." Said a gruff little voice.
"Yeah, but he's a 'he' so he'll probably get bigger." Another little voice replied.
 "Spruce what are you doing? Douglas and Yew get down from there!" A small but stronger voice scolded from somewhere farther away. The fog slowly cleared from Martin's vision.
Then a littler voice said from right up close, "Are his eyes supposed to be open?"
In that instant he saw her. She was tiny, about as high as the distance that Martin could spread his thumb and his little finger. She had delicate wings that were so thin and fragile they were transparent. Marin only saw them because of the rainbow sheen they gave off when the light hit them

just right. And then suddenly, she wasn't there.

"Hey!" Martin sat up quickly and searched the blankets. Then his head started spinning and he had to lay down again.

"Martin?" His Aunt Dottie came in. "Are you awake honey? Take it easy now, the doctor says you've had a mild concussion." She bunched up the pillow behind his head. "You're not to move too fast or get excited."

"Aunt Dottie?"

"Yes honey, you're at my house, safe and sound. Do you remember anything?"

"I...you were at the hospital?"

"That's right. Now don't be alarmed but you and your parents were in a car accident. Your mom and dad are still in the hospital so you're going to stay with me for awhile."

"Mom and dad?"

"Yes honey, oh...I'm sorry but there's no easy way to say this. They're in rough shape." She sat on the edge of the bed and took his hand. "The both of them are still in critical condition. We can go see them as soon as you've rested a bit more."

Even though Martin's head throbbed the tears welled up in his eyes. "No I want to see them now." He tried to get out of bed but his Aunt steadied him.

"Not right now dear, if you move around you could make your brain swell and it could...well it could be very bad indeed. Trust me Martin, you just need to rest. Your parents are in the best of hands. They are being watched every second by the amazing doctors at the hospital. Your grandfather is just down the hall from them so they're all together."

The thought of his grandpa in the same part of the hospital as his parents calmed him down. "Grandpa won't let anything happen to them will he?"

"Of course not honey, just like your parents didn't let anything happen to you. You're safe and sound, just a bump on the noggin." She tousled his hair. "Now, how about some tea?"

He nodded and she left. Aunt Dottie had a way of making the most amazing things seem normal and the most normal things seem amazing. Still, he wondered, had he really seen what he had seen when he woke up, or had he hit his head harder than the doctors thought?

***

Juniper stayed as still as a stone, watching Dottie and Martin from behind the leg of the dresser. The rest of her family had jumped down the vent shaft and were probably back in the Tamarack by now. *So that's him*, she thought, *the last of the Darragh family line.*

"Hey, nosey." Her dad's voice said from behind her. "Leave him be."

"Is he going to stay?"

"I don't know honey, he isn't ours." Her father turned to leave.

"But Dottie-"

"We are of the same clan," He jumped down into the vent shaft. "but Dottie is our charge, not Martin. Come on now." He waved for her to come down.

Juniper's wings only allowed her to fly for very brief periods. They were more of an aid to jumping from branch to branch. She used them now to jump down several feet into the shaft and then she stayed on her dad's heels. "But she's taking care of him, doesn't that mean that he's our charge too?"

"I suppose he is, but only as long as Dottie is looking after him."

"What about his Boughkin? Where are they?"

"The Darraghs were bringing their Christmas tree home when the accident happened." Her father pushed open a door made from a piece of duct tape that was supposed to seal a gap between the vents. "Perhaps the Darragh's Boughkin are still with the tree." He dropped to the basement floor.

"But how do we know?" She followed him. "What if they're hurt? We should go and make sure. Besides, what will become of their tree? It can't have given its life for nothing."

He stopped at the hole in the foundation that lead to the crawl space and then outside. "I don't know Juniper. All I know is that we are Dottie O'Neill's Boughkin, Christmas is almost here and that poor woman not only has her father in the hospital but her sister and brother-in-law as well." They walked through the dark crawl space, taking paths they had long ago made safe, and finally emerged outside. With a hard flap of her wings she followed her dad to a low branch on his tree. "On top of all that she now has to take care of little Martin. More than ever she needs our help to keep Christmas alive in this house."

That evening Juniper worried about Martin and Dottie. Even climbing into bed didn't make her feel much better.

MONTGOMERY THOMPSON

Chapter 2

The next day Martin climbed out of bed feeling much better. He quickly dressed and went downstairs to his Aunt Dottie who was baking in the kitchen.

"Well look who's up and about like a spring buck." Dottie said as she stirred a bowl of something dark and sticky.

"Is that Christmas pudding?" Martin said, smelling the pungent snap of nutmeg and brandy.

"Oh you're not so slow are you? Aye, Christmas pudding and a right big one too. I'm making a bunch of small ones for the relatives and neighbours and one whopper for us." She laughed.

Martin suddenly wished his parents were there to join in the excitement of Christmas. "Aunt Dottie, can we go and see mom and dad?"

"Of course dear. Just let me get this on to steam and we'll go see them."

Martin was quiet on the ride to the hospital. It made him nervous being in a car again. Some of the snow had begun to melt away, but the winter chill was still in the air. It reminded him of when he had pressed his face against the glass. That was when the truck had hit them. He scooted away from the window. Soon they were pushing through the doors of the large hospital building. Martin took the steps two at a time as he climbed up to the floor his parents were on.

"Now honey," Dottie knelt down to him. "they aren't awake yet and it might be a shock because they look kind of battered from the accident. Try not to be upset, everybody bruises a bit that's all."

Martin did his best to put on a brave face as he opened the door to his parent's room. They looked horrible. Both of their faces were black and blue and his mom's eyes were swollen shut. The oxygen masks made their breathing loud and the beeping of the hospital equipment just made matters worse. He couldn't stop the flow of tears as he stood between the beds and held both of their hands. He would give anything just to see them happy and laughing again like they were when they were heading home with the tree.

"There, there honey. It's okay." Aunt Dottie wrapped him in a hug. "It looks worse than it is. They're in goods hands here. We'll just keep saying prayers for them okay?"

Martin nodded and wiped away the tears.

"Would you like to go see your grandpa?"

He nodded again and Dottie gently guided him out of the room and down the hall.

His grandpa John smiled as soon as he came in. "Martin! Look at you, you're growing like a weed." Martin climbed up and gave his grandpa a hug. "Sorry about all this hospital stuff." His grandpa said. "They always make everything smell funny."

Dottie hugged her father. "How are you doing daddy?"

"Oh, you know…"

She just nodded sadly.

"Will you be home for Christmas?" Martin asked.

Hi grandpa tried his best to smile sincerely. "I don't know Martin. It's kind of touch and go right now. We'll see, okay? Let's just leave it at that."

Martin agreed. He had a feeling that the only option was bad news and he didn't need any more of that right now.

"So tell me, how is it living at your aunt's house?" His grandpa changed the subject.

"It's really nice. There's always good stuff to eat and there's little people I saw…" Martin clamped his mouth shut realizing he was about to give away his secret.

His grandpa looked at him with a sparkle in his eye. "Good things to eat huh? Well just don't eat too much of her good cooking. We'll end up rolling you out of there when it's time to go home."

They visited a little while longer before they had to go. When Martin gave his grandpa a goodbye hug the old man whispered, "Make your Christmas wish at the Tannenbaum. The wee Boughkin know what I'm talking about."

Martin's eyes went wide, but his grandpa winked at him to tell him to keep it secret. Martin quickly made a more serious face to cover up his excitement.

On the ride home Aunt Dottie took Martin's seriousness for sadness and promised to make an extra special dinner to cheer him up. When they got home Martin ran up to his room and shut the door. Once he was sure that his aunt was busy in the kitchen he stood on bed with his arms crossed.

"All right, I know you're there. My grandpa told me about you and the Tannenbaum, now show yourselves." He waited for second, then out of the corner of his eye he spotted a little movement down at the base of the dresser. And suddenly there she was again, a little girl only seven inches tall peered out from behind the leg of the dresser. In a blink she was gone.

"I saw you!" Martin dropped to his knees and searched under the dresser but there was no sign of her. "You're a girl aren't you? You don't need to be scared, I'm not going to hurt you or put you in a jar or anything." But no matter what he said she didn't come back. At least he knew she was real.

***

"You did what?"

"It was just for a second. He said his grandpa told him about us."

"Juniper everyone knows the word Tannenbaum, it's a famous Christmas song for crying out loud!" Her oldest brother Jack seemed to always be exasperated with her.

"Jack, just stay out of this." Her father cautioned.

"But dad she's-"

"I don't care, it's no business of yours."

"Why are you always protecting her?"

"Maybe when you have a daughter someday you'll understand." Tamarack told him.

Jack stomped off. "I'm never having a daughter."

Her mother Conifer came and sat down on the branch next to her. "Juniper, you have to understand that we are under oath not to interact with the humans. He depends on us to be discreet otherwise the whole system falls apart."

"I'm sorry mom, it's just that Martin's so…I dunno, scared. His parents are in the hospital and his grandpa is getting ready to leave. He needs a friend."

"Honey I know you mean well but believe me, nothing good ever comes from showing ourselves to the humans. Let Dottie take care of him, it's what she's good at."

***

That night, Martin saved his scraps from dinner and nonchalantly placed food under all of the furniture throughout the house. Dottie was engrossed in her TV show and had no idea what he was up to. Finally he kissed her on the cheek and went to bed.

The next morning he got up early and checked all the spots he had put food, sure enough, some of it was gone. Overjoyed he went into the kitchen and found Dottie baking away. He grabbed more scraps and replenished the supply. He spent the next few days observing the different places where he had put the food, but he never saw the Boughkin girl. Nonetheless, every morning there was always some food missing from at least one of the spots.

***

"Another mouse?" Conifer shook her head. "Where are they all coming from?"

"Mom, it's Martin," Jack said, "he's leaving food all over the place."

Conifer gave her husband a look that said he had better do something about this.

"Connie, I can't control everything she does. What are we gonna do, lock her up?"

"Lock who up?" Juniper bounded up a branch.

"You, you little freak show." Douglas teased.

"Douglas that's enough." Conifer scolded him, but it just fired up the others.

Yew jumped in. "I almost got bit trying to get that bread away from a mouse yesterday."

"Yeah mom, they're all over the place!"

"It's true honey." Tamarack said. "The shortcut through the south wall is completely overrun. I had to take the long way around."

Conifer had heard enough. "Well we'll just have to do our job then won't we. Are you Boughkin or are you bugs? You're the men, get out there and do something about it."

"But Martin wouldn't be doing this if I hadn't shown myself to him. I'll help get the mice out."

"No Juniper." Tamarack was firm. "You will stay here with your mother. Douglas and Yew. You-"

"Who? Me?"

"No, Yew...him...that one I'm pointing at...don't start this with me right now Spruce, I'm not in the mood!" Tamarack's needles were starting to turn yellow.

"Tam honey, calm down. He's just-"

"I know what he's 'just', dear and if he's not careful he's 'just' going to get a kick in the rear end. Now. Spruce, Douglas and Yew collect all the food and bring it to my tree. Then start around the kitchen and flush them out. Jack and I will take the corner exits at the southeast and northwest. Drive them to us and we'll get them outside. We'll make a food trail that leads them to the ditch by the field. Their burrows are all in there. No doubt they have families that are missing them by now."

They all went on their assigned duties. It took the better part of the day, but eventually they got all of the mice out of the house and sealed up the holes they had come in. Tamarack watched the last of his children climb up to the family branch of his mighty tree and settle in as they watched the last rays of the sun fade over the mountains. Juniper sat next to her dad.

"I'm sorry for all the trouble I caused. I didn't think-"

"No honey, you didn't. Now you know why such rules are in place. You need to understand that we are connected to our human families by oath and obligation. Saint Nicholas needs us to make Christmas work. Who lets him and his elves in the house on Christmas eve?"

"We do." Juniper sulked.

"Who does the reporting for the naughty and nice list?"

"We do."

"Exactly. We keep the spirit of Christmas alive. We are His magic. If the humans see us then they could explain the little wonders that happen all the time. That would mean that they wouldn't be wonders any more wouldn't it?"

"Yes sir."

"Okay then. We'll have no more of this showing ourselves nonsense then."

"Yes sir."

"Now, up to bed with you."

Juniper climbed up to her sleeping branch and settled in for the night. The stars twinkled in the Irish sky, forming shapes that only the Boughkin knew. She drifted off into a troubled sleep. In her dreams she saw the Darragh family Boughkin marching into a dark wood. They scrambled through the ruins of an ancient castle on the edge of a Lough. Something was chasing them and all the while a lone tree called out. It was the Darragh family Christmas tree, calling from where the car crash had happened. The Darragh Boughkin crashed through woods, fleeing from the sound and the darkness. It drove them into a deep gully until the were sliding, down and down into a bottomless pit.

"No!" Juniper sat up so fast she fell off of her branch and landed on the one below.

"Ow!" Spruce pushed her off of him. "What are you doing?"

"What's going on up there?" Tamaracks voice rose through the branches.

Juniper was in tears. "Daddy, I had a dream!"

Her brother's mouth dropped open. Boughkin never had dreams.

***

It had been days since any of the food had been taken. Martin was busy trying to devise another way to draw out the little Boughkin girl when the a loud bang from the kitchen made him jump.

"Aunt Dottie? Are you alright?" He called, but there was no answer. He ran downstairs and into the kitchen. His Aunt had dropped the phone and she was crying into her apron. Martin immediately feared the worst. "Aunt Dottie?"

"Oh Martin, I'm sorry. Don't worry, your parents are fine. It's grandpa. He's leaving us I'm afraid."

"No!" He ran to her and she wrapped him up in a hug. They both cried together for a little while. Then she stood up and dried her eyes. "We need to go and say our goodbyes."

It was a sombre ride to the hospital. Martin walked slowly up the stairs, dreading what was about to happen. As he came into the room a nurse was attending his grandpa. Everyone was very quiet. Even the air seemed to hold still and sounds tried not to make a sound. After Dottie spent a few minutes with him, talking softly and crying, his grandpa weakly waved a finger for Martin to come over.

"Grandpa?"

"It's alright Martin, we all have to make this journey. Actually, I am looking forward to it. It's a new adventure."

The tears flowed freely down Martin's cheeks. All he could do was nod.

"Martin...goodbye. I love you." The old man shook slightly and closed his eyes. Dottie sobbed as Martin stared at his grandpa. He couldn't be gone. Suddenly his grandpa's eyes opened slightly and with a mighty effort he whispered, "Use the wish...the carraig...and the tannen...baum." With a long sigh he finally passed away. His aunt rushed to the bed side as Martin stepped back and sat down. *Use the wish?* He thought. *What wish?*

Chapter 3

As they drove home Martin pondered his grandpa's dying words. The only part that was even vaguely familiar was the word Tannenbaum, but he still didn't even know what that was. He knew had to find that little Boughkin girl. Suddenly Dottie stopped the car. She was crying again.

"I can't do it Martin, not this year. Dad's gone and your parents are still in critical condition. There is too much going on. Christmas will just have to wait until next year honey."

It was hard to hear. Martin loved Christmas, but she was right. Somehow right now he didn't feel like presents at all. "It's okay. Maybe we can just have some Christmas pudding and watch a movie."

For some reason his aunt burst into a fresh round of crying. She reached over and hugged Martin. "You're such wonderful, sweet boy. Thank you for understanding." She wiped her eyes, smiled and nodded. "It's a good idea. Pudding and a movie."

***

"Pudding and a movie? That's a terrible idea!" Spruce ranted.

Tamarack paced with his hand on his head. "No, no…this is all wrong. She can't cancel Christmas. Times like this is when it's needed most!"

The other Boughkin children were stunned. Juniper felt that it was all her fault.

"I never should have shown myself to him. Now I've ruined Christmas!"

"No Juniper, honey it wasn't you." Her mother consoled her. "You have no control over deaths in the family." She looked at her husband who was still pacing. "Tam, I don't know how to fix this but it falls to us. We're the Boughkin here. We're the ones in charge of keeping the Christmas spirit alive in this family."

"I know Connie, I'm thinking!"

Suddenly Juniper knew what to do. "Daddy, I have an idea!" Tamarack stopped pacing and everyone looked at her. "Martin's Boughkin family needs us…and their tree, it needs us too!"

Tamarack rolled his eyes. "Not the dream again. We've been over this.

It wasn't a dream."

"Yes it was daddy! I know it was!" She slumped down on the branch, sobbing.

Conifer put her arms around Juniper. "Tam." She looked at him, pleading with her eyes for her husband to do something.

Tamarack couldn't withstand the power of Conifer's 'do something now' gaze. "Jack, you're coming with me. You boys start cleaning the property. I want this place looking so Christmassy the presents will sprout from the ground! Connie, you and Juniper start praying for snow." He kissed her and bounded down to the ground with Jack. Juniper followed after him.

"Daddy!"

Tamarack turned. "No Juniper, you can't go with us."

Juniper ran up and hugged him. "Thanks for believing me."

"Juniper, my little sapling, there is something I never told you. Martin's grandfather was a very special man. He saved your grandfather and our whole clan."

"Really?"

"Yes. A dishonest logging company was going to cut down the whole forest, but Martin's grandpa John tied himself to a tree and made them stop in their tracks. It was quite a standoff but John didn't back down."

"What happened?"

"Well pretty soon the police came, but so did the media. The whole operation was stopped until the courts decided what to do. So many people came out to protest that they ruled in John's favour. The logging company never came back. The Grand Meister granted John a Tannenbaum. Do you know what that is?"

"A wish tree!" Juniper was stunned.

"Yes, but the wish comes at a cost. The Grand Meister will-"

"Dad, come on!" Jack interrupted.

Tamarack smiled at Juniper. "He's right. I'll tell you the rest when I get back." He kissed her on the forehead and ran into the woods with Jack, leaving Juniper stuttering and stammering.

"B...but...what...the Grand Meister what?" She yelled after him, but he was out of sight. "Oh, pine nuts!" She kicked the ground. She needed answers and there was only one place to get them.

***

"Nuts! Definitely, more nuts!" Martin was helping Dottie in the kitchen. When she was stressed, Dottie baked. When she was happy, Dottie baked. Dottie just baked and right now Martin wanted to be there for her. So they made scones, potato bread, soda farls, muffins, cookies and cakes.

THE CHRISTMAS WISH TREE

It was late into the afternoon by the time everything was cooling on the counter and Dottie lay down for a nap. Martin sat in his room wondering what to do next when he caught a movement out of the corner of his eye. Ever so slowly he turned his head to look at the foot of the dresser. The little Boughkin girl stood staring up at him. Martin held his breath as she held her finger to her lips. He still hadn't remembered to breathe by the time she climbed up on the bed and put her hands on her hips.

"If you hold your breath any longer you're going to pass out. Then what good would you be to me?" Juniper said.

Martin exhaled. "You can talk?"

"Of course. My name is Juniper. I'm a-"

"A Boughkin! I know, my grandpa told me." He grew sad as he remembered his grandpa.

Juniper felt for him. "We're all so sorry to hear about your grandpa John. He was a hero to the Boughkin."

"Thanks." Martin didn't know what to say. Suddenly he remembered his manners. "Oh, my name is Martin."

"We know who you are silly! We're all in the same clan."

"We? How many of you are there?"

"In my family? There's me, my mom and dad and four brothers. One for each tree on Dottie's property."

"So, your like tree fairies?"

"Kind of. Some cultures call us dryads or sprites, some call us fairies or nymphs, but we call ourselves Boughkin."

"My grandpa told me to use the wish and something about the Boughkin, the Carraig and the Tannenbaum."

Juniper gasped. "My father just left with my oldest brother Jack to rescue your Boughkin family. Before he left, he told me that your grandpa saved our whole clan and was given a Tannenbaum wish."

"That's it! I knew you would know something about it! But what's a Tannenbaum wish?"

"I don't know. My dad said he would tell me more when he gets back."

"There's no time. My grandpa told me to use the wish...he must have meant that I'm supposed to use the wish to save my parents."

Juniper was crestfallen and flopped down on the bed. "I thought you might know what to do, but I guess you don't know any more than I do."

"My grandpa's last words were: 'use the wish'. I need to know more."

Juniper nodded and then had an idea. "I think I know where to look. It means I have to sneak up to my parent's branch and find the record needle."

Martin laughed. "You still listen to records?"

"No, the needle from the last Christmas tree. Every time you bring

21

home a Christmas tree we graft on a needle saved from the last one. The memories of every Christmas are stored in the needles."

"So a single needle remembers every Christmas I ever had?"

"No, every Christmas your *whole family* ever had, back to the beginning of Christmas. It's your entire family history!"

"Whoa." Martin was impressed.

"What we're looking for is on that needle." Juniper stood and bounded off the bed. "I'll be back in the morning to tell you what I found…that is if my mom doesn't catch me."

Martin didn't know what to say. Juniper was risking a lot just for him. "Be careful." Was all he could think of.

She stopped just as she got to the dresser. "Oh, and please don't leave any more food around, it attracts mice." With that, she was gone.

***

Juniper's heart was in her throat. Her family would be so mad at her. She shook it off. There was more going on here than any of them knew, she was sure of it. Grandpa John gave Martin the key to saving his parents, but that key wouldn't work unless she helped him. There was no way around it, she resolved to do what was necessary and that meant risking her family's wrath.

That night her father and Jack still hadn't come back, which made her next move easier. Before her mother went to bed, Juniper quickly jumped onto her parent's branch and searched the bark. In a deep crack she found the needle, hidden away and wrapped in a leaf. Tucking it under her arm she bounded up several more branches to a quiet place. She sat down and drew the needle out of the dry leaf, taking care not to crack it. She connected immediately with it, as Boughkin do to all living things. It only took her a moment to find what she was looking for. "Oh no!" She gasped. Quickly she put the needle back and hopped down to her parent's branch. With the needle safely back in it's hiding place she went up to her branch to get some sleep. When her mother called for dinner she replied that she wasn't hungry and stayed in bed. After awhile her mother came up to check on her.

"What the matter sweetie? Not feeling good?"

Juniper just hugged her mother tightly.

"Oh, you're worried about your father and Jack? They're alright. Your dad is very strong and brave. He'll be back soon, you'll see."

Something about her mother's tone wasn't very convincing. Juniper could tell she was worried. She hugged her tighter, then said goodnight. More than anything, she needed her rest now.

THE CHRISTMAS WISH TREE

***

In the middle of the night Martin woke to a strange sensation. A sharp pain was bothering his nose.

"Hey, Wake up."

It was Juniper. She was standing on the night stand tossing pebbles at him, which Martin found strangely funny and started laughing. Juniper looked at him like he'd lost his mind. Martin pointed at her. "You're standing...on the night stand!" he giggled.

"Yeah. Funny. Now get up, we have to go."

"What? Now?"

"Yes, now!"

"But why?"

"The needle showed me that we have to find my grandfather Cedar. He's the Grand Meister. He awarded your grandpa a Tannenbaum wish which is a big, big deal."

Martin rubbed his eyes and swung out of bed. It was all a bit confusing. "What exactly is a Tannenbaum?"

"Tannenbaum is German for 'Christmas tree'."

"But we're Irish. Why is it German?"

"Saint Nicholas, duh! That's where Christmas started!"

"Oh." It was news to Martin. "Wait, so Saint Nicholas is...?"

"Santa Claus! Which is Dutch for 'Sante Klaas' which means Saint Nicholas. Don't they teach you anything in school?"

"Sorry, geez." Martin started rummaging around for his clothes, not entirely sure if he wanted to go anywhere with this grumpy fairy.

Juniper continued to explain. "To the Boughkin, The Tannenbaum is the life of a tree given for a wish. It's very rare that a Tannenbaum wish is given. So rare that we only think of it as a legend." She jumped up to the high dresser so she could look him in the eyes. "Martin, you are the heir to a Tannenbaum wish! When the wish is made, the tree dies and the wish is granted, but it can only be used by placing it in the roots of the Tannenbaum tree on Christmas Eve. That's tomorrow night! If you're going to save your family, we have to find my grandpa so he can tell us where the Tannenbaum tree is."

"But I...I can't just leave!"

"You have to Martin. When the bearer of a Tannenbaum wish dies before using it, the wish gets passed to the youngest living member of the family, that means you. Now come on!"

Martin sighed. It looked cold outside and he was still so sleepy, but then he thought of his parents laying the hospital. If this was really the only way to help them then he would do it. He found his clothes and quickly got dressed. As he pulled on his coat he still wasn't sure that he was doing the right thing. "But Aunt Dottie-"

"She'll be fine, she has my mother and three brothers to look after her." Juniper said as she made her way down the hall. "Now you have to be very quiet."

Martin tiptoed to the front door and carefully pulled his boots on. He grit his teeth as he tried to work the latch quietly. It made a small click which made him pause, but then he opened the door and stepped out into the night.

"Shut the door, careful now." Juniper told him.

The door closed with another click and Martin ran after Juniper. "Wait up!" He hissed.

Chapter 4

"Wait up!" Jack called. Tamarack was well ahead of him and stopped to let Jack catch up. "Geez," He panted, "You're fast for an old stump."

"Old stump? Jack, I've still got hundreds of years ahead of me."

"Who let's trees live for hundreds of years these days?"

"Well, I can always hope."

"Good luck with that."

"Come on, we still have a long way to go."

"Wait dad. There's a better way." Jack launched himself up the trunk of a tall birch, scampering through the branches like a monkey. He stopped at a nest high up in the bare branches. After a minute he called down. "Come on dad he wants to talk to you."

Tamarack just shook his head and began climbing. When he got to the nest he hauled himself over the edge and came face to face with a large raven.

"This is your son?" The bird clucked at him.

"Yes. We're very sorry for the intrusion." It was impossible to read the bird's expression. He didn't have one. It was why Tamarack didn't like dealing with them.

The raven turned it's head and blinked. "It is not uncommon for the Boughkin to request transport in times of great need. Still, we must make sure that the birds do not become the pack animals of the fairy folk."

"Certainly not sir." Tamarack assured the bird. "We coexist in harmony and service to each other."

"It is our view as well. Your son tells me that you need transport to a far destination for a very noble cause."

Tamarack raised an eyebrow at his son. "He did? Yes, well he's right."

Jack beamed proudly.

"What is this noble cause?" Clucked the raven.

Tamarack sighed. "An entire family of Boughkin, some of our relatives, were in a terrible accident. We believe that their lives are in danger."

The crow blinked at him blankly. "Lives are in danger every day in the world."

"Yes, but there is more." Tamarack explained about the accident, the boy and the Tannenbaum until the crow stopped him.

"If what you say is true then the situation only involves a small group of individuals. Still, Saint Nicholas is a dear friend to our kind and as long as we have him in common, then we shall help you."

"Oh thank you!" Jack gushed.

Tamarack bowed. "The Boughkin of Darragh owe you a debt that we will happily repay whenever you wish."

"We will not forget. Now, what is this great distance that we must carry you?" When Tamarack told him, the crow laughed. "That is no great distance! I thought you meant that we would be crossing continents. It will only take us twenty minutes as I fly." The crow gave a loud call and soon another crow landed on the edge of the nest. They clucked at each other several times then the crow settled on the floor of the nest with his wings open loosely. "Climb on, but don't step on my wings." Tamarack carefully straddled the bird's back. The crow directed him to shift forward, then back and then how and where to grip. Jack was next. Finally they were all settled. "For small creatures you Boughkin certainly have some weight to you."

"My wife is a fine cook."

"Yes, it would appear so. Now, hold on." The crow spread his wings and dropped off the branch. Soon they were sailing over the countryside. Tamarack had never seen anything like it.

"You are truly blessed creatures to be able to live life in the air." He told the crow.

"We are all blessed in our own way." The crow replied.

They rose to a great height and surveyed the land below.

"There." The crow said. "I see signs of an accident."

"I can't see a thing!" Jack cried, holding onto his hat.

The crows began to circle down, not having the heart to dive as it would terrify their already fidgety passengers. As they descended, Tamarack could make out the crash site. There were tire tracks and some trees had been badly damaged.

The crows touched down and let them off. "We leave you to your fate, whatever it may be and bid you farewell." Then they bounded into the air and were gone.

Tamarack scanned the trees. "There are all kinds of creatures in these woods Jack. Some of them aren't very nice so I want you to keep your eyes peeled while I search the crash site."

"You got it dad." Jack climbed up to a low branch and began scanning the area.

Tamarack circled the site for clues, but there was no sign of any Boughkin. At the edge of the woods he found the Darragh's Christmas tree.

"Well?" Jack called down. "Find anything?"

"They're not here, but the Christmas tree is. I have no idea what we're going to do with it. It's far to big for us."

Jack dropped down and trotted over to his father. "Maybe not."

"What do you mean?"

"Hang on, I'll be right back." Jack ran off into the woods.

"Jack, be careful, there are badgers in there for crying out loud!" Tamarack shouted after him.

Several minutes passed while Tamarack paced, waiting for his son. Finally Jack emerged, floating in the air as he came through a low hanging pine bough. "Ta-daa!"

"Jack, what are you doing? Get down from...there..."

The fur covered head of a young buck deer appeared directly underneath Jack. He was riding it. Tamarack was stunned.

"Meet William. He's going to help us." Jack said proudly.

"William Hedgebounder at your service." The deer gave a bow and sent Jack tumbling. "Oh, sorry."

"Jack, what are you thinking?" Tamarack helped him up. "You can't just commandeer all the animals of the forest."

"Why not? William here said he would help."

"Yes! I will help!"

Tamarack looked at the young buck. "Wha...Why would you help us?"

"Because Santa's reindeer always help!"

"But you're not-"

"Dad! Can I talk to you for a second, in private?" Jack pulled Tamarack into a huddle. "I kind of told him that-"

"Jack-"

"Maybe-"

"Jack-"

"We could put in a good word for him."

"Jack!"

"Aw come on dad. He wants to be a part of the Christmas team." Jack winced.

Tamarack's needles were turning yellow and this time Conifer wasn't there to calm him down. He was about to scold his son severely but then he looked at William who was eagerly watching them. The deer was a little too cheerful. Suddenly he felt for William and he cooled down. "Okay William, we could definitely use your help-"

"Yes!" Jack sighed.

"But! There are no guarantees of a reward of any kind. Giving only becomes Christmas giving if it is given freely, with no expectations attached." He glared at Jack. "Many people forget that important fact this time of the year." He looked back to the deer who was still grinning at him. "So no promises, okay?"

William nodded casually then resumed grinning at them.

"What is wrong with him?" Tamarack whispered to Jack.

"I don't know dad, just go with it."

Using holly vines, they lashed the tree to the deer's meagre antlers.

"I try to grow them, but they never get any bigger than this." William said glumly.

"They'll do." Tamarack told him.

Suddenly William brightened. "That's the nicest thing anybody ever said to me!"

"Wow. Really?" Jack remarked. "I'd hate to hear the worst thing."

"Oh that's easy. Every morning my mom used to say, 'William, today you will be eaten by wolves.'"

"Okay, that's pretty terrible." Jack said. "Where is your mom now?"

"I think she was eaten by wolves." William started pulling the tree as Tamarack and Jack sprang to his back.

Tamarack whispered to Jack, "I don't have the heart to tell him that the last wolves in Ireland died off in the late seventeen hundreds."

"Really?" William said. "Then she must still be alive!"

"Oh, no William I meant that-"

Jack laughed. "You heard him?"

"Oh yes. Deer have some of the keenest hearing of any animal." William said with a hint of pride. "We can't see very well, but our ears make up for it."

"I'll have to remember that." Tamarack elbowed Jack.

"What else can you hear?" Jack asked.

"I can hear the squirrels and the huge storm that's coming this way and the birds and the-"

"Wait. A storm?"

"Oh yes. It's a big snow storm."

Tamarack looked at Jack. "I asked your mom and Juniper to pray for snow. I didn't think it would work so quickly. Hurry William. If we get caught in this storm it will make our job much harder."

***

"He's out there right now fighting for his life!" Aunt Dottie was inconsolable. She had called the police as soon as she found Martin missing. Usually they had to wait for twenty-four hours before filing a missing person's report, but the officers remembered her from the car accident and came out as soon as they heard about it. They stood at the door trying to calm her down.

"Please Mrs. O'Neill, try to breathe. I'm sure wee Martin is fine. Young lads can take to roving sometimes. I'm sure he's just lost in the woods or something. Can we come in?"

"Oh, yes, how rude of me." Dottie tried to dry her eyes. "Please come in gentlemen."

"I'm officer Sean, this is officer Pat." The two were nearly the same size; as tall and as wide as the door.

"I'm sorry boys. I'm such a wreck." Dottie let them in.

"Actually, I'm a woman. Patty. Officer Patty." The big policewoman shook Dottie's hand and took a seat.

"Oh dear. So you are, nice to meet you both."

Officer Sean was in the kitchen eyeballing all of the fresh baked goods. "Do you make these all yourself?"

"Oh yes officer, help yourself. There's jam and butter there on the island."

"Missus O'Neill-" Officer Patty began.

"Oh just Dottie please."

"Right. Well Dottie, can you tell us, when was the last time you saw Martin?"

Dottie filled them in on all the details. When she had finished, the two officers searched the surrounding outbuildings and the property line. They came back inside as the sun was going down. Officer Sean tucked into another scone while Officer Patty talked to Dottie.

"Well here's what we know. It looks like he left sometime between when you went to bed and when you discovered him missing. He changed out of his pajamas so at least we know he has proper clothing on. We're still trying to figure out why there are small pebbles on his pillow. Did he have a friend close by?"

"No. He's only been here a short time and there are no children in the area to speak of."

"Usually, in the case of runaways, the children have a friend that they runaway with." Officer Sean showed Dottie the stones. "These pebbles could be evidence."

"Oh dear." Dottie started crying again. "Why would he run away? He has nothing but love here!"

"The boy has been through a lot." Officer Patty said. "He just lost his grandfather and both of his parents are in critical condition. It's not your fault. No matter how much love you have shown him, this still isn't his home."

"Oh the poor, poor dear. And here I am crying all the time and going on so."

"Officer Patty is right. It's not your fault Dottie." Sean looked at Patty who nodded in agreement. "The good news is that we have a hunch as to where he might be."

"Where?" Dottie brightened immediately.

"We think he might be trying to get to the hospital."

"Yes. That makes sense. Oh why didn't I think of that?" Dottie began to cry again.

***

"Has anyone seen Juniper?" Conifer asked the boys. They all looked at each other and shrugged. "Are you telling me that not one of you has seen your sister this morning?"

"She went to bed early last night, that's the last I saw her."

"Well then Spruce, you take your brothers and find her. Martin has gone missing and there is...oh no." Conifer put the pieces of the puzzle together. "She's gone with him!"

"Oh she is so busted." Yew said to Douglas.

"Mom look, the police." Spruce reported from a higher branch.

"Boys come with me." Conifer hopped down the limb and entered the house through a secret entrance at the corner of the front porch. Just under the china cabinet they watched the exchange between Dottie and the police. Conifer knew she had to act quickly.

"Spruce, you and I are going to go with the police officers to the hospital. Douglas, you and your brother stay here and take care of Dottie."

"But mom!" Yew whined.

"But nothing Yew. I'll be back before you know it. Besides, someone needs to be here when your father comes back to fill him in. Now you both know what to do. It's your time to lead the family. Don't let me down." She gave them both a kiss, then took Spruce by the hand and headed out across the carpet, up the arm of the chair and into the pocket of officer Patty's coat. Yew and Douglas looked up at her as the officers stood and prepared to go. Conifer leaned out of the pocket, blew them a kiss and said, "You'll do great!"

***

"You're doing great William, keep going!" Jack cheered him on.

"Helping is harder than I thought it would be." William grunted as the tree got stuck on rocks and soft spots in the ground.

"Jack get down there and try to keep the tree free of snags. I'll stay up here and keep him going in the right direction."

Jack jumped down and began pushing on the tree every time it got caught. Tamarack climbed to the highest point on William's stubby horns to try and get a better view. "Oh no. Nothing but bog for miles." He groaned.

"Dad wait!" Jacks voice sounded far away.

Tamarack looked back. Jack was face down in the mud while William and he were getting farther away. "Whoa William! Stop. Take a breather."

Jack caught up to him and climbed onto William's back. "I don't ...think I can...keep this up." He panted.

"My head hurts."

Tamarack sat down. "I know William. You did great, you both did. Let's take a little rest then see what energy we have left. Maybe we can make it to that road over there."

"Road?"

"Yeah, it cuts through the bog. Roads are very dangerous, but we'll have to chance it."

"What's a road?" William asked.

"You don't? I mean...it's a thing that humans drive their cars on."

"What's a car?"

"Really?" Jack was incredulous.

"Humans use them to travel at great speed. They're very dangerous. Many deer get hit and die every year because they didn't know what a road or a car was." Tamarack gave Jack a look that said 'have a little sympathy.'

"Then I should know so I can live! I must see this road." William got up and began pulling the tree through the bog.

Chapter 5

"We don't want to go through the bog." Juniper said from a low branch. "We'll have to go around."

"Where are we going?" Martin complained.

"Grandpa John said something about the carraig right? Well the word 'carraig' is Gaelic for 'rock'. The Boughkin can use ancient standing stones to locate other Boughkin. I have to find my grandfather, so that's where we're going."

"To the carraig?"

"A carraig, yes. There's an ancient site on the other side of the bog. We'll have to circle around it. You don't want to get caught in the bog in winter."

"Okay, just go fast. I'm freezing!"

As nature spirits, Boughkin didn't feel the cold. Juniper looked at him curiously then thought, *it must be a human thing*. She lead him along game trails around the bog. By the time they reached the far side, the sun was going down.

"There it is Martin, look!"

An old, worn stone stood in the middle of a clearing in the woods.

"Wow, it looks magical."

She smiled with a twinkle in her eyes. "It is." Fluttering up to it, she put her hands flat on the rock and concentrated on her grandpa. A moment later her eyes flew open. "I know where he is, and your family's Boughkin are with him!"

"Really?"

"Yes Martin, they're all safe! Oh thank goodness. Come on!" She bounded up to his shoulder. "You're much faster than I am. I'll point the way."

Martin headed into the woods on barely perceptible trails. As the night closed in around them it grew much colder and the wind began to howl in the branches.

***

The pocket of the police coat was stuffy but Conifer and Spruce kept quiet and managed to dodge Officer Patty's hand when it strayed in. Finally they ascended the stairs to the floor where Martin's parents were. The officers inquired about the boy, but none of the night nurses had seen him. They were shocked to learn that he had run away and promised that they would keep an eye out for him. Then the officers walked down the hallway to Martin's parent's room. On the way, they passed the room where Martin's grandpa had been. The flowers were still on the windowsill. Conifer's attention was drawn to a small framed box among the vases. It held a single sprig of Cedar.

"I'll be back." She leapt out of the pocket and ran into the room. Spruce just watched her go, feeling helpless to do anything but wait.

Conifer scrambled up a steel stand and managed to catch the window ledge. She dangled by her finger tips but the rounded edge and the paint were too slick to hold onto. She was going to fall when suddenly, she was lifted up.

"I've got you mom." Spruce had somehow managed to get onto the radiator and pushed her up to the ledge. She climbed up the rest of the way then reached down to help him. Finally they were both standing safely on the window sill. Conifer looked at her son proudly. "You're growing up."

Spruce blushed slightly then changed the subject. "So what did you take off for?"

"This." she walked over to the cedar sprig. It was enclosed in a wooden frame between two pieces of glass.

"What is it?"

"It's a promise, and I think it will tell us what we want to know." She put her hands up against the glass and closed her eyes. It took all of her concentration to penetrate the glass, but finally she connected with the cedar sprig. "Oh my goodness!"

***

"Oh my goodness, it's getting so cold." Martin jammed his hands in his pockets.

"Maybe you should put up your hood." Juniper tugged it into place. "Does that help?"

"Yes, thank you."

"You know, you're not at all like I thought you would be."

"What do you mean?"

"I thought a human child would be, I don't know, small and not able to do anything for themselves."

"Well everyone is like that for a couple of years. But then we get older and we can take care of ourselves better. The only thing is, our parents don't think we can so they constantly tell us not to do this and not to do that."

"My parents are exactly the same. My father tries to keep me from doing anything."

"Well he's not keeping you from doing anything now."

"That's true. I just hope that what we're doing is the right thing."

They trudged on through the woods. Soon the woods became even darker as the storm howled around them. As Martin squinted through the darkness he saw a massive shape looming up through the trees.

"What is that?" Martin said through chattering teeth.

"It's an old castle, or what's left of it. That's where we want to go. We should see a lake soon."

"I hope it's warmer in there than it is out here."

"Are you going to be okay?"

His teeth chattered. "You don't feel c-cold?"

"No. I'm not really sure what that means."

"You mean don't get cold?" He asked again, not believing what he was hearing.

"I don't think so. Is that why you're vibrating?"

"Yeah, humans get cold. We can die if we get too cold."

"You didn't tell me that. Hurry then, get to the castle! My grandfather will know what to do with you."

Martin tried to hurry down the path, but it was so dark he couldn't see. Juniper had no problem seeing in the dark and directed him as he stumbled blindly holding out his hands in front of him. Soon he felt the rough stone of the castle and Juniper began calling out.

"Grandfather! Hello? Grandfather Cedar are you here?"

"In here child." The old voice sounded like a rocking chair was playing the cello. "Come out of the storm."

"Reach up Martin." She directed. "Now duck underneath that, watch your head."

Suddenly the wind stop blowing him around.

"Juniper! My little sapling why have you brought this human child here?" The grandfather sounded upset.

"It's young Martin Grandfather, the grandson of John. John has passed away and now the Tannenbaum wish belongs to him."

Grandfather Cedar sighed. "And he has come to use it."

"Yes Grandfather. Can you help?"

He sighed again. "Yes child, but all is not as you may think. Still, a promise is a promise. Here give him this." Cedar handed a flask of amber liquid to Juniper who passed it to Martin. "Go on, it will warm you."

"What is it, some k-k-kind of m-magical potion?" Martin eagerly pulled the stopper and chugged several mouthfuls of the liquid. It burned his throat and filled his sinuses with a smoky sharpness that made his cough it out through his nose.

"What's the matter boy? You never had whiskey?"

"Grandfather!"

"No sir." Martin spluttered, his nose burned and his eyes watered.

Grandfather Cedar waited for Martin to stop his gasping and then said, "Well, are you warmer or not?"

Martin tried to keep from throwing up as he nodded. He was definitely warmer, but he didn't feel very good.

"Grandfather, human children don't drink whiskey." Juniper snatched the bottle away from Martin.

"More for me then." Cedar took it from her.

"Grandfather you have to tell us where the Tannenbaum tree is. He needs to make the wish tonight."

"I know child, don't be impetuable...impetu...oh don't be pushy! I'm sure young Martin here will get his toy or whatever it is that he wants so badly."

"He doesn't want a toy! He's trying to save his parents lives!"

"What's that?"

"His parents are dying in the hospital from a terrible car accident and his grandfather just died. Grandfather, you have to help us!"

"Oh dear...well that's horrible. Why didn't you say so? Go straight out that doorway and up the hill. It's a mighty climb, but I believe you can make it. When you get to the top you will see it. The standing stones of Crann Nollag and in the center is the Tannenbaum tree. You've got to go now. The storm is closing in, and around here the snow brings the lightning. Go!"

***

"Go William! One last pull! That a boy!" Jack cheered him on as William pulled the tree onto the road.

"What is this?" He panted.

"This is the road William."

"It's so easy to walk on, so smooth."

"Don't get too fond of it, as a matter of fact, avoid it at all costs."

"But why, it's so nice." William clopped around on the black tarmac as snowflakes started to fall around them in the swirling wind.

"Imagine another deer, but much larger than you, running full speed and hitting you."

"That would hurt."

"Now imagine that that deer is made of solid rock."

"A deer made of rock? I want to meet him."

"No William, there is no deer made of rock it's just an analogy."

"Dad, car's coming."

Jack and Tamarack bounded into the bog and hid behind a gorse bush, but William just stood, staring at the oncoming vehicle.

Tamarack stood up and yelled at the deer. "William, Get off the road now!"

"Um, dad?"

"Not now Jack. William! Move – your - butt!" Tamarack called out, but the deer didn't move.

"Dad, um, that car is moving really slow."

It was true. The headlights ambled around the bend accompanied by a rumbling and rattling noise. Slowly the vehicle came to a halt in front of William who stood transfixed by the headlights.

"What's wrong with him?" Tamarack whispered.

"You keep asking me that. I have no idea." Jack responded.

The tractor door opened and an old farmer stepped out. "Easy boy. Looks like you got caught up in some vines." The farmer cut the vines from the tree and William sprang away. "Now what do we have here? Will you look at that? By thunder it's a perfect Christmas tree." The farmer rolled the tree into the bucket on the back of the tractor and headed off down the road.

Tamarack walked out onto the road and watched him leave. "No, no, no. We can't let him take the tree, not after everything we've been through."

"No dad we can't."

"No we can't." William said from behind them.

Jack jumped back. "William! What happened to you?"

"What do you mean?"

"He means that you just stood there." Tamarack was as surprised as Jack. "That tractor almost ran over you."

"What tractor?"

"I don't think he remembers." Tamarack suggested. "It must be the headlights. They mess with his head."

The two Boughkin hopped onto the deer's back. "William, you hear that rumbling noise off that way?"

"Yes I do."

"Catch us up to it and you'll finally see a tractor!"

The deer gave a mighty leap and sprang off across the bog.

"William!" Jack shouted against the wind. "You're really fast!"

"I know! I'm a deer!"

William closed the distance on the tractor quickly.

"He's heading the right way at least." Tamarack struggled to hold on.

"You mean William?"

"No, the farmer, look. His farm is over there, and just over that hill is home!"

Tamarack and Jack clung tightly to William's horns as the deer bounded up to the rear of the tractor. The farmer turned around, shocked.

"What in the name of-"

William bounded into the back of the open cab. For a moment the world exploded into a mass entanglement of arms, legs, hooves and yelling. Then, suddenly all was calm. The three of them were piled in a ball on the tractor's seat and the farmer was nowhere to be seen.

"Where'd he go?" Tamarack looked around.

"He must have fallen out." Jack offered, untangling himself from William's horns.

"Ooh fun! I've never been in one of these before." William started pushing buttons and pulling levers. The windshield wipers stopped, the lights went off and the tractor lurched into a higher gear, sending it speeding past the farm and up the hill.

Chapter 6

"They're going up the hill!" Conifer pulled her hands away from the glass.

"What hill mom? What are you talking about?"

"This cedar sprig is from your grandfather's tree. He just told me that Juniper is with Martin."

"You can do that?" Spruce looked at his mother with renewed admiration.

"No, only a Grand Meister can. Listen, Juniper took Martin to see your grandfather Cedar. Martin's grandfather was given a Tannenbaum wish by your grandfather, now it belongs to Martin and he's going to use it to save his parents."

"What?" This was all too much for Spruce. Magic from his grandfather and legends about wishes coming to life. "When?" Was the only question he could think of.

"Tonight. We have to get those police officers to Crann Nollag. Come on!" She leapt to the curtain and slid down to the floor with Spruce on her heels.

"Wow mom, your fast."

"Yeah..." she said eyeing the surroundings. "I've been at this while. Spruce, you see that big jar of petroleum jelly up on the shelf there?"

"Uh huh."

"Do you think you can push it onto that table by the hall window?"

"I can try."

"Go, and hurry!" Conifer climbed up the table and grabbed a cotton swab from among the cleaning bottles and paper towels.

Meanwhile Spruce had managed to get to the shelf in the tall cabinet next to the table and was putting his shoulder to the jar. "Man, where is Jack when you need him?"

"Spruce, you're just a strong as Jack. You don't give yourself enough credit. Now come on, give it everything you've got." Conifer encouraged her son.

Spruce planted his feet and gave a mighty shove. The plastic jar suddenly broke free and skidded across the shelf. "Look out mom!"

Conifer dodged the heavy container as it dropped onto the desk. The lid popped off as it bounced and finally vibrated to a stop. "You did it!" She dipped the swab into the petroleum jelly and started writing on the window that looked out onto the hall.

"Mom, the cops are coming back down the hall." Spruce could see them from his high vantage point on the shelf.

Conifer finished writing and wrestled a can of foaming window cleaner into place. "Spruce, jump on the button."

Spruce suddenly understood what she was trying to do. He aimed carefully and leapt down onto the button on top of the can, sending a spray of cleaning foam at the window. The can toppled over and they both went tumbling into the trash can.

Officer Sean was confounded. Both he and his partner were sure the boy would have gone to the hospital, but there was no sign of him. After interviewing some of the nurses they headed for the stairs at the end of the hall.

"His grandpa just passed, in that room there." Officer Patty said. "He wouldn't be in there would he?"

"It looks like their cleaning – hey." Officer Sean jumped back. At that moment the spray hit the window.

"Would you look at that." Officer Patty exclaimed. "Now what would make that happen?" She flipped on the lights in the room, picked up the can and began looking at it.

Officer Sean immediately saw the writing. As he puzzled over it's meaning a nurse walked up behind him. "It's Irish. It means Christmas tree."

"How in blazes did it get there?"

"I don't know officer. The last ones in here before the cleaners was the family. Unless of course you believe in fairies."

"I don't madam." Officer Sean was adamant.

"Sean look." Patty held up the cotton swab. "All the tools are here for little hands to do their work."

"Now Patty don't you start with all your fairy nonsense."

"The little people are real Sean. I've always said so, and now here's your proof."

Sean groaned. "I believe in facts and things that will hold up in a court of law."

Officer Patty gave the nurse a knowing look. "Well the antics of the fairy folk won't hold up in a court of the law, but I think they're telling us where wee Martin has gone."

"To a Christmas tree? What is that supposed to mean?"

"No Sean. Crann Nollag is an ancient hill fort not far from here."

Officer Sean seemed to suddenly remember it. "Ach! Right. I took my son there last summer. I'm going daft."

Patty held up the swab and gave him a look he was all too familiar with.

"Okay, you win. We'll go to the Crann Nollag, but I'm telling you. It's no place for a boy to be climbing about, especially in this weather. If he's there, then he's in trouble."

"I'll get an ambulance to meet you there." The nurse said and scurried off to the desk.

While the three had been talking, Conifer and Spruce crept out of the trash can and climbed into Officer Patty's coat pocket.

"I'm so glad the only thing in that trash can was paper towels." Conifer dusted herself off. Just then Officer Patty started running. They both crouched down in the corner of the pocket and held on.

***

Martin crouched down and held on as another gust of wind buffeted him. The storm grew stronger as they climbed. It seemed that the weather was centered on the hill itself, with the sole purpose of knocking him off of it. Shivering from the cold, he gripped a rock on the steep slope and pulled himself up.

"Juniper!" He yelled into the wind and snow.

"I'm right here Martin, keep going!" Her little voice was right next to his ear, but he could barely hear her against the howling of the storm.

Just keep putting one foot in front of the other. He thought. *One step at a time.* It was as much as he could manage, but it was something. His face was numb and he had lost feeling in his hands, but he kept on. At last the steep slope began to flatten out. Minutes later they staggered against the wind that howled and swirled across the top of the hill. Through the blinding snow and darkness he could see the outlines of tall stones, beyond them a monumental tower rose into the sky. It was the tallest tree he'd ever seen.

"It's the Tannenbaum!" Juniper yelled. "Martin, you have to put your Christmas wish underneath it!"

Martin pressed up against the tree to hide from the wind. "But I don't have anything to write with." He cried.

Juniper thought for a moment then said, "Pull some of the bark off of that tree over there."

"What tree? I can't see a thing."

"Okay, I'll get it. You dig around in the roots here. Grandfather said that there are a lot of lightning storms up here. There should be some burnt charcoal on the ground. Find some, even a tiny piece. I'll be right back." Juniper bounded off into the storm.

Martin clawed at the ground with his frozen hands. Every effort stung with pain but he kept searching. He dug a hole under one of the roots as deep as his hand and suddenly they came out black. He reached in again and pulled out a charred piece of wood. Wrapping his hoodie around him for the hundredth time he huddled in the crook of the tree, shivering. By the time Juniper got back to him he was fast asleep.

"Martin!" She yelled into his ear but he barely stirred. She kept yelling. "Wake up! You have to finish it!"

Finally his eyes cracked open. "So...cold..." He mumbled.

"Martin, here's the paper." She shoved the piece of birch bark into his hands. "Write!"

He grasped it and struggled to sit upright. A fog clouded his mind. All he could hear was her voice and the wind, and the knives of cold biting him.

"Martin you must write! For your grandpa... for your mom and dad!"

The thought shocked him into action. He bent down and forced his numb fingers to grip the charcoal and form letters. When he was done she pulled his cold ears and urged him on.

"Now fold it. You have to address it to Santa."

He struggled to push the thick paper into a fold and scribbled 'To: Santa' on the outside. Suddenly he knew what to do. Just go home. He stood and took several shaky steps as he tried to walk off the hill. He could see his house, warm and inviting. It was Christmas. Aunt Dottie's pudding and mom's Christmas dinner.

"Martin! Where are you going? Come back!" Juniper pulled at him, trying everything to get him to turn around, but he wouldn't give up. Finally she pulled hard on his right ear which made him turn in a circle, stumble back toward the tree and fall down at the roots. The letter tumbled from his hand, landing just inches away from the hole he had dug. Juniper stared at it. It was so close. She could push it in, but it had to be him. She buried her face in Martin's coat and began to cry.

***

"Hold on!" Jack cried.

"I can't see. Am I dead?" William said.

"No, we're all very much alive. Now push some of those things you pushed before. See if you can get the wavy wand thing going again."

William kicked at the dashboard. The emergency flashers came on and miracle of miracles, the wiper started up.

"Yes! You did it William!"

"I did it! What did I do?...Oh look, a tree!"

"Dad, we're going to hit that Alder!" Jack yelled. "Everybody jump

THE CHRISTMAS WISH TREE

out!"

"No wait!" Tamarack said. "I've seen this done. William, wedge your hooves into these points on the wheel here, and here." He pointed. "Jack, get up here and hold onto the wheel." Tamarack jumped up on the small strip of dashboard and grabbed the wheel. "Now, everyone turn the wheel this way."

William and Jack saw what he was doing and helped. The tractor lurched to the left.

"Woo hoo!" William hooted. "Bye bye tree!"

"Focus everyone. We're not there yet. Now come back this way." Tamarack continued to call out directions as the tractor lumbered out of the bog and down the far side of the hill towards Dottie's. Soon the house came into view.

"Um dad, how do we stop this thing?"

Tamarack was pulling levers and flipping switches frantically. "I don't know!"

"Turn the wheel!" Jack said as they bore down on the house.

"I can't!" He heaved on the wheel. "William, get off of the wheel!"

William's legs had dropped through the holes in the steering wheel and he was laying on top of it, his face pressed up against the windshield.

"Thith ith unformthortable." He sputtered.

The tractor exploded through the hedge and clattered into the garden. The only thing that stood between them and the house now was a small earthen berm.

"Thith ith going to hurt!" William cried.

They braced for impact but the tractor bounced hard over the berm, launching into the air. When it came down it bounced into a turn sending William, Jack and Tamarack tumbling out onto the lawn. They picked themselves up and stared in amazement. The tractor was chugging off into the bog as the Christmas tree rolled to a rest at the steps of Dottie's porch.

Dottie heard a rattling noise over the howling wind and looked up from her tears. A loud bang and what sounded like shouting came from the front yard. She jumped up and went onto the front porch. She couldn't believe her eyes. There on the lawn was a perfectly cut Christmas tree and a deer grazing peacefully in the middle of the raging blizzard. Suddenly it dawned on her.

"Oh what a fool I am! Cancelling Christmas just when it's needed the most!"

***

The police car skidded to halt in the parking lot of the Crann Nollag historical site. Officer Sean began looking for footprints or any clue that Martin had gone up the mountain, but Officer Patty marched straight up the trail.

"Patty! For crying out loud, will you slow down."

"I will not Sean. That boy is up there, now come on. It's time to work off Miss Dottie's scones."

The two officer's powerful flashlights pierced the darkness as they pushed up the hill through the storm. Conifer and Spruce looked out from the pocket.

"See anything mom?"

"No Spruce, nothing yet. They-"

Just then a lightning strike lit up the woods. The sound was so loud it drove the officers to the ground.

"Lord Almighty!" Sean exclaimed.

"That hit the top of the hill. Let's go!" Officer Patty took off at a run.

Chapter 7

"Martin! Wake up please!" Juniper held Martin's face and pleaded.

Somehow it was enough, but when his eyes fluttered he didn't see Juniper. His grandpa stood at the tree. Martin reached out to him, his fingers stretching out across the snow covered soil. As he reached, the tops of his fingers pushed the letter toward the hole he had dug. It teetered at the edge for a moment, then toppled in. All around them lightning lit up the sky and the snow swirled in the howling wind. With a bone shattering crack a massive lightning bolt connected with the tree. It seemed to glow, then it exploded into a million pieces showering them with wood and bark. Slowly, the giant cedar tree came crashing down around them.

***

"Martin!" Officer Patty called.

Conifer and Spruce jumped out of her pocket. Conifer stopped short as they reached the fallen tree. She started to cry. "Father..."

"Mom, I found them!" Spruce called from inside the wreckage of the tree.

A moment later Juniper came out, leaning on her brother who delivered her safely to Conifer's waiting embrace.

"Mom?"

"Oh my brave little sapling. You did it! You saved Martins's parents!"

"What's wrong mom?"

"This tree."

"I know, it was magnificent wasn't it?"

"More than that sweetie. It was your grandfather's tree."

"What?" Juniper finally understood. Her grandfather was the Tannenbaum. He had given his life that two others may live. *No wait.* She thought. *Martin's grandfather too. Two lives for two lives.*

***

The bright sun shone in the window as Martin awoke. He was at his Aunt's house but something felt different. *Was it all a dream?* He wondered. The smell of brandy, cinnamon and nutmeg filled the house. Martin sprinted downstairs and stopped short. Piles of presents all wrapped in gold paper sat beneath a beautiful Christmas tree sparkling in the corner.

"Aunt Dottie!" Martin ran into the kitchen. His Aunt was there, baking away.

"There he is, oh my dear boy!" She swept him up in a big hug. "How are you feeling?"

"I'm fine!"

"It's incredible that you didn't get killed when that tree fell on you."

It was real? It was all really real!

"I'm so grateful that you're home safe and sound. And speaking of safe and sound Martin I have the most incredible news." She handed Martin a plate of cookies, hot from the oven and a cup of tea.

"Cookies for breakfast?"

"Oh it's a special day in every way. Now sit down so I can tell you the news."

Martin plopped down on the big chair in front of the fire.

"Your parents woke up last night. They have completely recovered. The doctors can't explain it. They call it a Christmas miracle! Officer Sean and Patty are bringing them here as we speak."

Martin couldn't believe it. His wish had come true.

Just then the front door opened and two large police officers came in, grinning from ear to ear.

"It certainly smells like Christmas in here." Officer Sean said, heading to the kitchen. Officer Patty came straight up to Martin.

"Hello Martin. You gave us quite a scare. I'm Patty."

"Nice to meet you sir." Martin held out his hand.

"Actually, I'm a woman," She shook his hand and smiled. "but that's okay, most people make the same mistake." She moved aside as Martin's mom and dad came in the door. Martin ran to them, his heart bursting with joy.

Later that day, after all of the presents were opened and everyone was stuffed full of Dottie's magnificent cooking, Martin went outside. A buck deer with a regal rack of antlers grazed on the lawn. Martin approach it cautiously.

"My aunt told me you've been here since last night. Are you a friend of the Boughkin? Anyways, I know you had something to do with what happened. I just wanted to say thank you. Stay as long as you like, you're always welcome here."

The deer looked at him, slightly bowed it's head then turned and went on grazing.

"Martin!" A little voice came from the big Tamarack tree by the fence. Martin ran over.

"Juniper?" He ducked under the branches and looked up into the canopy of the big tree. There, on a branch the same height as Martin's head, sat the little Boughkin girl.

"Hi! You look way better than you did last night."

"Juniper! We did it! My wish came true!"

"I know! Isn't it wonderful! There are a few people I'd like you to meet." One by one, other Boughkin appeared on the branch. "This is your Boughkin family. They take care of the Darragh's, always have, always will. Meet Ash, Beech, Yew, Larch, Elder, Maple, Apple-"

"Yeah, just like Gwyneth Paltrow's daughter!" The little Boughkin exclaimed.

"And Durian." Juniper finished.

"He's a foreign exchange student from Mal-a-laysia." Young Maple said, struggling with the pronunciation.

"I'm so honoured to meet all of you." Martin bowed.

"The honour is ours young Martin. Because of your special relationship with Juniper and the nature of your grandfather's status, and now yours, we are permitted to show ourselves to you." Ash was clearly the father and came forward to look Martin straight in the eye. "But you must never tell anyone about us. Our duty is to you and your family, but all Boughkin serve a higher ward; that of Christmas itself, and everything, and…" he glanced up at the sky. "…every One, that presides over it."

"I understand perfectly sir. I promise I will never tell."

"Thank you. That is most reassuring. We must go now and return to your home. Dottie's Boughkin will take care of things here. We will be there waiting for you when you return. Oh, one more thing. I wanted to say thank you, to you and Juniper and all the Boughkin of Dottie O'Neill. You saved our lives and honoured the Tannenbaum. Special blessings will follow you all the days of your-"

"Dad, that tractor is back!" Jack interrupted. Suddenly Juniper's family appeared on the branch next to her.

Tamarack waved. "Sorry Martin, we'll do introductions later. Right now we've got to help that farmer." He flew down off the branch and ran into the bog with several Boughkin in tow.

Out in the bog, the tractor bounced along on it's own and behind it ran the farmer, trying to catch up.

"William! I think we're going to need your help!" Tamarack called.

The buck sprang into action, scooping up the Boughkin in his huge antlers and bounding out into the bog as Martin and the Boughkin laughed under the branches of the old tree.

ABOUT THE AUTHOR

Musician, kayak guide, renaissance swashbuckler…Montgomery Thompson likes to do fun stuff. Born in Maryland and raised in Colorado, Monte claims Sandpoint, Idaho as his hometown; which is kind of confusing but hey! Ya gotta be from somewhere, right? Even more perplexing is that most of the time he can be found in the hills of Northern Ireland playing a tune, writing a word and buckling a …swash? Hmm, that is odd now isn't it?

His other works for kids include *The Shielding of Mortimer Townes*. For the grown-ups and fans of sci-fi action adventure be sure to read Montgomery's premiere works; *The God String* and *Augmentia*

All of these are, of course, available on Amazon.com and Amazon.co.uk

Printed by Amazon Italia Logistica S.r.l.
Torrazza Piemonte (TO), Italy